# Clotilda's Magic

by Jack Kent

**SCHOLASTIC BOOK SERVICES**

NEW YORK · TORONTO · LONDON · AUCKLAND · SYDNEY · TOKYO

To Junie

ISBN 0-590-31247-2

12  11  10  9  8  7  6  5  4  3  2  1          11          9/7  0  1  2  3  4/8

Printed in the U.S.A.

"Nobody wants a fairy godmother nowadays,"
said Clotilda. She sat down on a daisy to feel sorry
for herself in comfort.

Tommy and Betty were
picking flowers.

"There's a bug on this one!"
said Tommy.
"I'm not a bug!" said Clotilda.
"I'm a fairy godmother!"

"You're a bug!" insisted Tommy.
"Don't be rude," Betty scolded.

"I don't believe in fairy godmothers!" said Tommy.

"I don't believe in little boys who don't believe in fairy godmothers," said Clotilda.

"I refuse to argue with a bug!" said Tommy.

"Whose fairy godmother are you?"
asked Betty.

"Nobody's!" said Clotilda, and she
began to cry.

"Crybaby bug!" mumbled Tommy.
"If you're a fairy godmother," he said,
"let's see you do some magic!"

Clotilda dried her eyes, blew her
nose, and waved her magic wand.

She waved her magic wand at a polliwog . . .

and it turned into a frog.
"It would have done that
anyway," said Tommy.

She waved her magic wand at an acorn . . .

and it turned into an oak tree.

"It would have done that anyway,"
said Tommy.

She waved her magic wand at a caterpillar . . .

and it turned into a butterfly.

"It would have done that anyway," said Tommy.

She waved her magic wand at Tommy . . .
and he turned into a donkey.

"He would have done that anyway," said
Clotilda. "The world is full of magic and
anyone who can't appreciate it is a donkey!"

And Clotilda sang a little song:

"It's magic when the sun comes up,
To light and warm the day.
There's magic in the rainbow
When the clouds have blown away.

"It's magic when a flower blooms.
It's magic when it's snowing.
  It's magic when a robin sings,
And when the grass is growing.

"There's magic in a spider's web
(I marvel at the art of it).
The world is full of magic
And it's magic that we're part of it."

"That was lovely!" said Betty.

"Thank you," said Clotilda, bowing.

"For my next act I'll grant you three wishes."

"If you can make wishes come true,"
said Tommy, "why don't you grant your own?"
    "It only works on other people,"
Clotilda said sadly. "What's your first wish, Betty?"

"I wish Tommy was Tommy again," Betty said.

"Granted," said Clotilda, although she thought it was a waste of a perfectly good wish.

"And I wish I would grow up to be
as nice a lady as my mother," Betty said.
"Granted," said Clotilda.

"She would have done that anyway," mumbled Tommy. And he hurried away before anything else could happen to him.

"One more wish," said Clotilda.

"I wish . . ." said Betty. "I wish that you could be my own personal fairy godmother for always."

"Granted!" Clotilda said joyfully. "That was MY wish, too!"

So they both lived
happily ever after.
Although . . .

. . . it's just possible
that they would have done that anyway.